dixi
books

S. C. Farrow

S. C. Farrow has been a writer and editor for over twenty years. She's worked on everything from educational texts to novels. She's also written and produced several films including a feature-length psychological drama. Based in Melbourne, Australia, she has a Master of Arts degree in Creative Writing. She occasionally teaches creative writing at various Melbourne institutions.

Open Wounds

Australian Short Stories

S. C. Farrow

Dixi Books

Copyright © 2019 by S. C. Farrow

Copyright © 2019 Dixi Books

Open Wounds - S. C. Farrow

Proofreading: Andrea Bailey

Designer: Pablo Ulyanov

Cover Design: Federica Aglietti

Printed in Bulgaria

I. Edition: May 2019

Library of Congress Cataloging-in Publication Data

Farrow, S.C.,

ISBN: 978-619-7458-41-1

1. Fiction 2. Adult Fiction 3. Short Stories 4. Australia

© Dixi Books Publishing

46 Harrier Mews, SE28 0DQ London, UK

info@dixibooks.com

www.dixibooks.com

Open Wounds

Australian Short Stories

S. C. Farrow

dixi
books

The Voice of the New Age

Contents

Preface

The stories in this collection have been developed over a very long time-almost twenty years. Some of them are inspired by events that occurred in real life. Others are entirely fictional.

The characters in these stories exist in different locations and periods in time. They have vastly different lives, yet they are all connected by the devastating effects of physical and/or emotional trauma. Everything about a person, from the way they think, remember, learn, how they feel about themselves and others, and the way they view and understand the world, is affected and shaped by their experience.

Open Wounds is a collection of unflinching Australian short stories that shines a light on those moments in life that are as profound as they are traumatic.

Barbie Doll Bitch

'You're out!' Patricia shouts.

'I am not!' Craig yells back as he runs like crazy to the next base.

Through the window I can see them laughing and having fun while I stand there, numb, waiting to talk to the Barbie Doll. I take a deep breath as I look inside the classroom and see her sitting at her desk sipping coffee as she reads. She's got a red pen in her hand, so I guess she's looking at our morning math test. I count my steps as I make my way forward, three, four, five, six. If I count, I can't chicken out. I focus on her black hair, teased to the ceiling, and swallow hard as her perfume, sick and sweetly, crawls up my nose and down the back of my throat. If I can push it down into my stomach, I'll be okay. If I don't, I might be sick.

'Why aren't you outside, Merryn?' she says, looking up at me with black-rimmed eyes.

'I want to sit next to Sandra,' I blurt out, wondering how she can keep her eyes open at all, with all that stuff on them.

She leans back in her chair as she looks at me, trying to figure out what I'm up to. 'You already sit next to Patricia,' she says.

'I know. But I want to sit next to Sandra.'

Her eyes widen in their black-rimmed sockets and I think they're going to bug out of her head.

The next day, I reach over to get the handkerchief from Sandra's pocket. 'Shhh,' I whisper as I take it. I don't want the Barbie Doll to see us. I never want the Barbie Doll to see us.

Sandra isn't like the rest of us. She's different. Special. She doesn't look weird or anything like that. It's just hard for her to learn things. And she doesn't talk much. I don't think she knows too many words, but she talks to me 'cause I listen and let her say what she wants to say without losing my temper or making her hurry. Her eyes are swollen, and her cheeks are streaked with dirt and tears. 'Supersonic, idiotic, disconnected, brain-infected dumb-bell...' That's what they chant whenever she's around. She doesn't know what it means, but she does know what a punch feels like. I wipe the smear of snot from her cheek. Luckily, the Barbie Doll is scratching something on the blackboard. While she can't see me, she can't embarrass me, and she can't embarrass Sandra. I give Sandra back her hanky. Her long thumbnail scrapes my hand as she takes it. I love Sandra's hands. Her skin is fine, like an expensive pair of gloves. Her fingers are long with manicured nails. Pretty hands. Not like mine. And she's always so clean. Her long golden hair is always so neat in a ponytail. Her mother must love her very much. The Barbie Doll has fingernails like Sandra's but hers are red, blood red, just like her lips.

After lunch, I get a fright when Sandra slips her hand into mine. I didn't know she was behind me. 'C'mon,' I say, leading her up the corridor. 'Let's hurry up and get inside.'

But it's too late. The chorus begins: 'Supersonic, idiotic, disconnected, brain-infected dumb-bell. Supersonic, idiotic...' And Kerry corners us at the classroom door. She looks down at our hands. I whisper to Sandra to go inside and sit down. 'Whaddya hang around with her for?' Kerry demands as she watches Sandra go.

'You leave her alone,' I snap.

Kerry shakes her head. 'You're dumber than she is.'

'Yeah, well, she's my friend.'

Kerry shrugs and walks off.

She is my friend. And I don't need them.

In the classroom, a nasty smile twists the Barbie Doll's mouth as she walks up and down the rows between our desks. I sit down quietly, praying she doesn't see me. 'Everyone is to write a poem for their homework,' she says, stopping beside our desk. My heart pounds in my chest. I hold my breath and wait. 'Everyone,' she says, 'except for Sandra.' I sneak a peek at Sandra drawing in her picture book. Her thoughts are someplace else, far, far away from the apes and the hate that makes her cry. We all know that the Barbie Doll hates her. We overhear her telling the other teachers that Sandra should be in special school, that being here is a waste of time. At last, she walks off and I can breathe again. 'The topic can be anything you like,' she says, 'but it must be ten lines or more and it must rhyme.'

I wish *my* thoughts were someplace else, someplace safe. But that's not going to happen. It's never going to happen.

It's Monday morning and we sit at our desks drinking milk made warm by the early morning sun as we stood in the playground singing *God Save the Queen* in honour of some lady we don't even know. But I know the days are getting longer and that soon it will be Christmas time. I play outside until the sun goes down and my grandma calls me in for tea. I don't mind playing on my own, but Grandma says I need to make friends and that I really shouldn't be so shy. I don't know why.

I finish my milk and wonder where Sandra is. She's away today. I wish she wasn't. It's time to read our poems. The Barbie Doll knows I hate reading out loud and when no one volunteers she makes me go first.

'Go ahead, Merryn,' she says from the front of the room.

Fifty-eight eyes bore into me as I take my paper and leave the safety of my desk. I stand at the front of the room and shake while the Barbie Doll glares at me beneath her pitch-black beehive. 'You can begin,' she says.

I want to. I try to. But the words are stuck in the back of my throat, and the edge of my paper is wet from the sweat leaking from my hands. My ugly hands.

'Go ahead,' she commands.

Now the words on my paper blur through my tears and fear. You bitch. You fucking bitch. I'm not allowed to say that at home, but I know what it means and that's exactly what she is.

Later that day, a tennis ball rolls to a stop at my feet as I sit at the edge of the playground. 'Nice poem, dopey,' Craig says as he chases after it. 'Sure Griggsy didn't write it for ya?' Craig is the most popular boy in our grade. All the girls love him.

'No,' I say, 'She didn't write it for me.'

'Come on,' Patricia puffs as she runs up beside him. 'Whaddya doing? Get the ball.' Then she turns to me. 'Where's your shadow today?'

'I dunno,' I say with a shrug. It's true. I don't know. I hope she's back tomorrow.

'You wanna play?' she asks.

I look at her sideways. Do I wanna play? What does that mean? I'm suspicious, but yeah, I wanna play. I nod my head.

'Okay,' she says. 'Go on Trudy's team. They're batting.'

It's Friday today. The Barbie Doll's been away all week. So has Sandra. I miss Sandra, but I love playing rounders. I've played it every day. Maybe I shouldn't. I feel bad for having fun without her. I wish she'd come back.

All week, Miss Pearson, the substitute, had us making pink and white crepe paper flowers. Even the boys had to make them and today we finally learned why. At home-time, Miss Pearson handed out a notice.

Dear Parent,
Miss Clover is getting married at
St Stephen's Church
Bernard Road
Mooralla
on Sunday 24th September at 4pm.
She would like to invite all her students to attend the ceremony.
Sincerely,
Miss Pearson (substitute)

It's Tuesday today, which means the Barbie Doll is getting married next weekend. She hasn't been back to school at all so Miss Pearson is still our teacher. I like Miss Pearson. She doesn't make me read.

Sandra and I sit beneath the big oak tree in the playground. There was something wrong with her head but she's better now and back at school. 'S. A. N. N, Sandra, now put an N. Good. Now a D. Yep. Now an R. And now an A. Good, we're finished.' I hold up our gift, a horseshoe shaped bit of cardboard covered with white silky ribbon and decorated with pink ribbon roses and a card signed by both of us.

Sandra couldn't get the hang of winding the ribbon around the horseshoe, so I did that. She wasn't too good at making the ribbon roses either, so I did that too. It's the most beautiful thing I've ever made. Grandma bought the ribbon for me, but I did the rest. *We* did the rest. Miss Clover will love it, and I will be at her wedding to give it to her. As soon as she sees it, I know she'll change her mind about me and Sandra.

I miss rounders, but it doesn't really matter. Sandra's back and it's just me and her again. Lunchtime seems long today.

Today's the day. Sunday. Miss Clover's wedding day. The crepe-paper arches look beautiful all covered in our crepe-paper flowers. Sandra and I haven't been chosen to hold them, but we don't mind. We stand at the end of the line, our arms linked with the other kids and wait to give Miss Clover our gift. I'm so excited. We've been here for ages. We're not allowed inside the church. I guess we'd make too much noise. But I can't wait to see her. Then something happens. Two men in suits open the church doors and a man with a big camera hurries out.

'She must be coming,' someone says.

'She is coming,' says someone else. 'Look! There she is!'

Through the open doors, I catch a glimpse of her. Her eyes are still black, and her lips are still red, but today she looks different. Today, she looks like a princess. When the wind blows her veil the man she married stops it from covering her face then gives her a kiss on the cheek. I can't stop staring at her. She looks so happy. How can someone so happy be so mean? After they have their photo taken their friends throw confetti over them, a rainbow of paper rain that means it's time for them to leave. I grab Sandra's hand and make sure we're in the line on Miss Clover's side. We have to give her our gift. Miss Pearson instructs the others to raise up the wire arches, just the way she showed us. We giggle and cheer as Miss Clover and her husband walk under our crepe-paper tribute.

'Here she comes,' I say to Sandra, holding out our horseshoe ready to slip it over her arm as she passes. But she doesn't even look at me. And she doesn't look at Sandra. She holds her husband's hand as she walks right past us toward the big black car that's waiting to take them away.

Sandra rubs her eye as she looks at me and asks, 'Why didn't you give it to her?'

Tears fill my eyes as I push her away. It's all her fault. It's all her fault that the Barbie Doll picks on us. It's all her fault that the Barbie Doll hates us. And the others are right. She is dumb—and I hate her. 'I don't want to be your friend, Sandra. I don't want to be your friend.'

The stink of perfume is long-gone from the classroom. And I'm glad. Sandra hasn't been at school since I told her to get lost. That was three weeks ago. Miss Pearson said she wasn't coming back at all. The Barbie Doll isn't coming back either. I don't miss Sandra now. I hope she's okay, but I don't miss her. Me and Craig and Patricia play rounders every day.

Falling

A cutting gust of wind blows through the King's Domain gardens snatching breath from inside Olivia's mouth. Gasping, she's forced to stop and draw precious air back into her lungs. Russel doesn't notice. He walks on without her. As she breathes deeply, another gust swells so fiercely it wrenches foliage from the majestic elms that line both sides of the pitted pathway. Transfixed, her eyes widen as she holds out her hands to the leaves that begin to swirl all around her. Never in her life has she seen anything so beautiful. It's a breathtaking vortex where, for a single moment, time stands still, and she is alone with God. She knows this is His doing. That the leaves are a show just for her. Just for her. She hasn't been to church for a long time, but she knows He's watching her and that He hasn't forgotten her. Suddenly, the wind shifts and sighs and scatters the shattered leaves across the ground. It's a graceful swan song.

At last, she snaps out of her trance. When she looks up she realises Russell, with his shaggy blond hair, ice blue eyes, and a thumb hooked casually through the belt loop on his jeans, has stopped walking and turned to watch her. His look is hard. Not hard the way Graham looks at her with that stillness in his eyes and that anger on his lips. Even so, she doesn't dare move as eyes slide down the length of her body and back up again. She doesn't know what he's thinking. She doesn't know what he might say. Then without a word he turns away and keeps walking.

She swallows the fear that's balled up in her throat and hurries to catch up with him. She should be on her way home, not trailing behind Russell as he makes his way to the Music Bowl. The others went home after the movie, but he didn't want to go. He wanted to hang out more. She wanted to hang out too. She knew her mother would worry, but then again, she probably wouldn't.

As they round a sweeping curve in the path, she spots the Sidney Myer Music Bowl nestled in the garden's lush undulating slopes. A magnificent outdoor performance venue, the aluminium canopy looks like a sheet of white fabric elegantly draped over two giant vertical poles. Russel heads straight for the back of the building where the massive steel cables supporting the awning come together like strands of hair in a pony tail before disappearing into a concrete anchor buried deep in the ground.

She watches as he leaps up onto one of the strands. What the bloody hell is he doing? He glances back as if to ask if she's coming. She hesitates. Is he crazy? Then casually, as if he does this kind of thing every day, he starts walking the tightrope towards the Bowl's oblique roof.

Shit. What's she going to do? She looks left and right, then glances back over her shoulder. There's an old couple coming this way. She looks back at Russell. He's almost made it half way. Without thinking, she throws her leg over the nearest cable and straddles it as if it were a horse. She hauls herself up and stands precariously on the twisted steel. Buffeted by a gust of wind, she begins to wobble. She flails her arms as she tips further and further to the side. Her left foot slips off the curve of the cable. Then finally, with the threat of a hard fall looming, she tips back the other way. Balance restored. She takes a moment, and a big deep breath, then slowly, carefully, inches her way along the cable towards the back of the canopy.

At first, the climb up is nothing. Easy peasy. Like walking up the hill at the end of her street. Then all of a sudden, it gets steeper and harder to climb. Russell kind of crouches as he scrambles to the top, but she has to do it on her hands and knees. At the top, she lies on her stomach and stays perfectly still, too terrified to move. Beside her, Russell snorts and snuffles. The sound disgusts her, but she doesn't say anything. He moves closer to the edge and leans over. What's he doing now? She inches as close to the edge as she dares. From the top of the Myer Music Bowl, she expected to see a lot more than she can see. There's nothing except the Shrine of

Remembrance and a few tall city buildings. Then she looks down. Oh, shit. It's so fucking high. The skin over her knuckles becomes as thin as tissue paper as she clings in a death grip to the edge of the canopy. The people in the seats below them…. They're so far away she can't make out their faces. Russell lets the gob of spit trickle from his lips. It dangles and stretches. It gets heavy and falls. She watches. Slow motion. It seems to take forever to hit the ground.

She wonders if that's how long it would take for her to hit the ground.

She wonders why boys always spit.

The end of her nose is numb. Goose bumps prickle her skin. She wishes she'd brought a jumper. She slides back a few inches and rolls onto her back. The sound of fun made by Sunday strollers dissolves in the autumn air long before it reaches this height. Except for the occasional squawk of a passing bird, the embarrassing heave of her smoke-choked breath, and the coursing of her blood in the back of her ears, it's disturbingly silent.

Two months ago, she saw ABBA play here. All the big acts play here, either here or Festival Hall, and if someone worth seeing does play here, you hope it doesn't rain and pray you can get close enough to the stage to see them. She doesn't tell anyone about Abba. They were cool for a while, but not anymore. She doesn't tell anyone about Carols by Candlelight either. For years, she'd trail behind her mother lugging blankets and baskets through these gardens, so they could sing carols by the light of a candle purchased to raise money for the blind. She still thinks about the irony of that. They stopped going the year they saw a teenaged couple fucking on the grass in front of them. The boy was on top of the girl, his skinny arse making hard work of it. They didn't make a sound. They didn't speak. They didn't moan. All they did was fuck. Graham's like that. He doesn't speak or moan when he fucks her. He just sneaks into her room and climbs on top of her when her mother's asleep. When he's done he warns her that if she tells anyone, he'll hurt her. She used to love Carols by Candlelight. Now, on Christmas Eve, they sit at home and eat potato chips and watch it on TV.

Russell rolls onto his back, pulls a scrunched-up cigarette packet from his jeans pocket, lights two, and passes her one. He gives it to her without even asking if she wants it. She swings around to lie on her back beside him. She watches the end of her cigarette burn a long shade of red as she drags on it. She likes smoking. She likes the feel of the smoke as it goes down into her lungs, filling obscure creases and crevices.

Russell turns onto his side and props himself on his elbow. He stares down at her. With those ice blue eyes. She can't believe she's up here alone with the most beautiful boy in the whole school. The wind blows a ribbon of hair across her face and causes her nipples to jut out beneath her t-shirt like gargantuan icons to her womanhood. For months when she'd been 'developing', her breasts had steadily swelled and ballooned. Her mother decided containment was necessary. One night after her bath, her mother stood in the doorway and stared at her with soggy maternal eyes. 'You're a woman now,' she said, whipping out a bright red spidery-looking thing from behind her back. She'd stared at it, totally mortified. This couldn't be happening. With nowhere to go, her mother had charged forward and plunged the elastic contraption over her dripping wet hair and snapped it into place on her chest. A training bra; no awkward clasps. Her mother stood there full of oohs and ahhs and doesn't it look lovelies. She stood there burning redder than the bra. But the earth declined to open up and swallow her, and God refused to smite her mother, so there she stood hoping death would come quickly to end the nightmare.

Now, Russell reaches out his man-sized hand, callused and scared by the weekends spent helping his carpenter father, and sweeps the ribbon of hair away from her face. He reaches down to her chest. She gasps as he splays his fingers over the mound of her breast and squeezes. She lies there frozen like a chicken, the same way she does when Graham touches her. She doesn't want to be a frozen chicken. She wants this to be right. She *needs* this to be right. The next thing she knows Russell is leaning over her, his eyes half closed, and his full pink lips puckered. She holds her breath as he presses his lips against hers. He wants this. He really

20

wants this. She presses her back against the canopy. She wants this too. She wraps her arms around his neck and tries to savour the moment. Russell flicks his half-burnt cigarette over the edge, then slides his hand from the mound of her breast to the mound between her legs. Despite the layer of denim between their flesh, she can feel the heat in his fingers. His fingers are strong and forceful. She wants this. He reaches up and pops the button on the waistband of her jeans. She wants this. He tugs at the zipper and pulls it down. She wants this. He slips his hand inside, slides it lower and lower down towards her secret. Suddenly, she grabs his hand and stops him. It turns out she can't do this. She can't do this at all.

Russell removes his hand and leans back to stare down at her. The look in his eyes is still hard, only now it's hardened by disappointment. Then starts the long slide down the canopy towards the ground.

He's not going to wait for her.

She lets the cigarette fall from her fingers then throws her forearm over her face as great gobs of sorrow begin ripping through her body.

She hates Graham. She hates her mother. She hates God.

She stops crying and wipes her eyes. As she stares up at the sky, she realises it's getting late and that she should be getting home. But what's at home? The usual Sunday night lecture followed by fish fingers, a bath, and a movie she's not allowed to watch to the end because she has to go to bed.

What will Russell go home to? Bet it's not fish fingers.

She sits up and looks down the length of the canopy. It's a long way down.

What would happen if she stood on the edge of the Bowl, stretched out her arms, and let herself fall? Would God's almighty hand come swooping down from Heaven to rescue her? Would he whisk her up for the 'what were you thinking?' lecture? She doubted it. It seems God's a bit fussy about what He hears and what He ignores. Some people say He's the answer to all their prayers. But He doesn't hear hers; He doesn't answer her prayers.

She gets up. She's awkward and ungainly but finally manages to get to her feet. She stands right on the edge of the canopy as the wind whips around her, blowing her hair and shaking her balance. But the view… She can see for miles. It's beautiful.

She holds her arms out to the sides and lets the breeze rock her.

What would her mother think of her standing up here?

What would Russell think?

She doesn't think he'd think anything.

What would her mother think? Or Graham?

Or God?

God can go fuck Himself.

Heat

She sits by the window skimming her tongue across her swollen bottom lip as she peers out at the sunburnt landscape through the near black lenses of her Best & Less sunglasses. They haven't said a word for over two hundred kilometres. Exhausted, she rests her head back on the seat, then gasps as her heart skips a beat. A highway patrol car is speeding up beside them, overtaking the bus. Her heart pounds in her chest as she turns away from the window and glances at him, sitting beside her in the aisle seat, headphones in his ears as he stares down at the backlit screen of the phone he grips tightly in his hand. He didn't see it. She breathes easily as she turns back to the window.

The only coach out of town, the bus had been pre-booked by twenty-seven elderly women on a grudge match visit to the Wallalaga Lawn Bowls Club. An event, apparently, not to be missed. One woman, decked out in white pedal pushers and a white short-sleeved Polo shirt, grips the back of the seats with knotted fingers as she makes her way down the aisle towards them.

He switches off the phone and quickly grabs her hand, forcibly weaving his fingers through hers in a slick show of unity. A picture of perfect happiness, he flashes the old lady a smile. The old woman narrows her eyes a bit as she smiles back and shuffles by.

When the old woman is safely gone, she looks down at her hand, at her fingers so tightly woven into his that her skin is white. She pulls her hand away and catches sight of the drop of blood on the frill of her off-the-rack blouse. She pokes at it, shoves it into the folds of the diaphanous fabric, then goes back to staring out the window.

The coach burns another hundred kilometres before finally pulling off the highway and into the carpark of a weather-beaten roadside café. She has no idea where they are. It's the middle of fucking nowhere.

The moment the driver kills the engine, the lawn bowlers are up, desperate for the bathroom and a cup of tea. He is desperate for a smoke. He pockets his phone, orders her not to take long, then bustles his way through the chock of little old ladies towards the door.

When he's gone, she plucks a compact mirror from her black vinyl handbag and checks her mouth. The skin is swollen and bruised, but the split has scabbed over. She grabs her tube of plum velour lipstick and spreads it over her lips. That will have to do.

At last she unfolds her crumpled legs and makes her way to the front of the coach. At the door, the heat is like a slap in the face. She stands on the bottom step and looks around at the landscape. In every direction, as far as she can see, the scorched blue sky drips into the withered brown horizon. The heat haze is like a soft-focus filter. Nothing seems sharp or in focus. She knows some people have a connection to this land, but she doesn't. It's nothing like her homeland in Western Ukraine with its fertile plains and chains of mountains that stretch for miles across the open landscape. A Ukrainian bride, she was betrothed to him when he travelled to her country on a 'Romance Tour'. Two of her friends had already come here. She wanted to be happy like they were.

She takes two deep breaths then steps out of the airconditioned comfort onto the pavement and heads over to join him. He narrows his eyes and sucks on his cigarette as he turns around to look at her, then without a word, he flicks the cigarette away and heads inside the roadside café.

Inside, aged yellow paint flakes from aged plaster walls, tattered curtains hang from sagging rods, and rattling ceiling fans stir the leaden air. He flings her twenty bucks and tells her he's going for a piss then leaves her alone to queue for food behind the busload of little old ladies.

Behind the counter, two overweight women with pendulous breasts and limp hair hanging beneath cardboard hats stand, tongs in hand, ready to serve up a disturbing array of deep-fried delights. Sausages in batter, fish in batter, hamburgers in batter, fried chicken, pork fritters, dim sims, crab sticks and mysterious squares on sticks. All come, of course, with a side dish of soggy chips.

She tugs at the collar on her blouse. She never noticed before how it rubs the back of her neck. As she hides the bloodstain, she catches sight of a fly. Caught in the slipstream of the swinging front door, it lunges at crumbs spilled on sills and dives at sticky pools on the floor. It's only a matter of time before the ultra-violet beauty of the bug zapper beguiles it. The insect version of the electric chair, it'll fry for being a filthy little pest.

The last to reach the counter, she orders food for him and coffee for herself. As the women sling food, they share a joke and laugh at the punchline. As she watches them, she can't help but wonder about their lives and the choices they made to end up here. She can't remember the last time she laughed.

One of the women thrusts a plate of deep-fried food at her and says they'll bring her coffee to the table.

She takes the plate and weaves her way through the labyrinth of old ladies seated at the café's laminate-topped tables. She can feel their eyes on her, watching her as they murmur and speculate. She pushes her sunglasses up higher on her nose as she strides defiantly towards the table by the window where he sits and waits.

Once there, she slides the plate of food across the table in front of him and takes a seat. He upends the bottle of tomato sauce as she plucks a packet of cigarettes from her handbag. He glares as she lights one up and reminds her that he's eating. She looks at him as she tilts her head to one side and drags on the cigarette, drawing smoke deep into her lungs and leaving a cheap plum velour lipstick kiss around the filter. He frowns at her and scoffs, then bites down on a sauce-soaked deep-fried crab stick.

A cup and saucer rattle with the approach of a teenaged waitress, a stick figure in a uniform five sizes too big for her. She keeps her eyes down as the mousy-haired girl slides a cup of coffee onto the table in front of her then, as indifferently as she'd arrived, slinks away without a word.

She turns back to the window. The sun burns through the tattered curtain, sears her fingertips as she presses her fingers to the glass. She rests her head on the back of the seat and stares at the ribbons of colour shimmering above the tarmac. A dribble of traffic passes by on the highway. Her eyes drift as she wonders who they are and where they're going. More importantly, where is she going? Where are they going? And what's going to happen when they get there? Another new life? Another new beginning? She bites her lip. She doesn't think so.

She couldn't believe they'd paroled him. She'd moved on, got a good job, and was saving to buy a car. She'd warned him not to come back. But there he was, the day he got out, standing on her doorstep begging for her to let him in. She'd attempted to shut the door, but he'd pushed his way in and sworn it wouldn't be for long. As usual, she gave in.

Time had begun to alter her face, but his face, some five years older than hers, had become thin and drawn. His jet-black hair was hard against his sallow skin. Crow's feet, long and deep, seemed like they'd been stomped into the edges of his eyes. And shadows, dark and unsettled, had dug into the hollows above his cheek bones. She couldn't help but pity him. She thought she could help him, thought she could heal his pain…

It wasn't long before he was staying out all night. He wouldn't tell her where he was going or how long he'd be. He'd just demand money and warn her not to ask questions.

When he came home, he'd slip into bed beside her and stroke her hair with a gentle hand and kiss her with a loving mouth. He'd whisper in her ear and tell her that when he was in the nick, all he could do was think about getting out and coming home to fuck her. When he was done, he'd order her out of the bed and into the shower. He didn't want to sleep with her when she stank like sex.

When he told her to go to the gym she was surprised. Confused. She wasn't stick thin, but she certainly wasn't heavy. He told her that he wanted her to look nice. Not for others. For him.

One night, she came home late from work. Rage bristled in the back of his eyes as he sat on the couch and demanded to know where she'd been. She told him she had to stay back at work. He demanded to know who else was there. Other men? He didn't want her hanging out with other men. In fact, from now on he didn't want her talking to other men. She knew the answer didn't matter. He flew off the couch and snatched a handful of her hair. She reached up and grabbed his wrists and begged him to stop, but he wouldn't let go. He dragged her backwards along the hallway. 'Who are they?' he demanded. 'Who are they?'

Inside the bedroom door, somewhere between the bed and the wardrobe, she heard a noise that sounded like a thump. And felt the crack. She bit the side of her tongue and drew blood. She couldn't save herself as she stumbled to the floor. He hadn't hit her with a fist since he'd broken her jaw.

She sat there, trembling, with her eyes closed and just breathed. Her shoes were off, left somewhere down the hall. Her pantyhose were torn. Her skirt was rucked up around her thighs. 'You're mine,' he growled as he grabbed her arms and hoisted her onto the bed, 'you understand? You're mine.' Then he straddled her hips and held her down as he wrapped his hands around her throat. 'And you'll do what I tell ya,' he seethed, his eyes bulging with rage, 'you understand?' Tears welled in her eyes as he glared at her, glared *through* her, like she wasn't even there. She couldn't get any air. Her heart hammered in her chest as her head swelled like a balloon. She clawed at his arms and tried to then pull him away, but he clenched his jaw and tightened his grip even harder. Tears rolled down the side of her face as she looked at him, begging him with her eyes to let her go.

Then, as her fingers tingled, and her body turned cold, something snapped in him. He let her go. He released his grip and sat back. Just like that. As she clutched at her throat and gasped for air, he bent down to kiss her and stroke her hair as he whispered, 'I'm sorry,' over and over again. He wept and whined that it wasn't his fault, that *she* made him do it, that *she* was to blame. She threatened to leave him and never come back. He held her tight and whispered that if she left him, he'd find her. He'd hunt her down, he'd find her, and he'd kill her.

Now, she looks at him sitting on the other side of the table.

Sweaty and anxious, he'd come home this morning as she was getting ready for work. His clothes were torn, and his knuckles were bloody. She knew better than to ask why. As she stood in front of the mirror buttoning her blouse, he'd scrabbled around in the dresser drawers and told her they were leaving. She'd frowned as she'd told him she was running late and that she didn't have time for his bullshit. Furious, he clipped her across the lip with a backhander that sent her into the mirror, shattering it for seven more years of bad luck. Blood dripped from her split lip as he grabbed her wrist and dragged her through the front door.

Suddenly, *crash, bang, clink, clatter!* Startled, he jumps in his seat and snaps his head around as a tray of dirty dishes hits the floor. The stringy-haired waitress covers her mouth with her hand and dances on her toes as she looks down at the mess.

He exhales as he dumps his knife and fork on the table. His appetite is gone, vanished in a fit of the jitters. She stabs the cigarette out on the saucer beneath her cup as she exhales a mouthful of smoke, then tells him she's going to the bathroom. He warns her not to be long—and to get him coffee on her way back. She grabs her handbag, walks around the overwrought waitress and heads for the ladies' room.

The same aged paint flakes off the walls and the tiles, once pure white, are now cracked and riddled with mould.

She peels off her sunglasses and slowly raises her eyes to look at herself in the mirror. The bruise around her eye is fading, but the bruise on the side of her mouth has spread like a grotty smear of Vegemite. She wets a paper towel and pats at the perspiration glistening on her forehead. It's so bloody hot. She can't wait to get back on the bus.

Suddenly, a toilet flushes, then another, and another, as three old lady bowlers walk out of the stalls and stand beside her at the row of sinks. As the old women chat and run water to wash their hands, the smell of department store perfume encircles her, wends its way into her nostrils. It reminds her of her grandmother. She smelled exactly the same way. She reaches for her sunglasses and slowly slides them back on her face. When the old women are done, their looks of curiosity harden into pity or indifference, depending on the story they've made up about her, then walk out the door leaving her alone. She doesn't care what they think. It's none of their business. She fishes out her tube of lipstick and fixes her face as best she can, then heads back inside the café.

As she steps out of the bathroom, she catches sight of something in the corner of her eye. Her heart starts racing as she turns to look. Two uniformed cops are coming through the front door. She holds her breath and glances through the front window. Sure enough, the highway patrol car that sped past them on their way here is parked a few short metres from the bus. She slides her eyes over to him at the table. He shakes his head, almost imperceptibly, warning her not to do anything sudden. Not to do anything stupid. She looks back at the cops, smiles slightly as she stops to let them pass, then quietly goes back to her table.

She takes her seat beside the window, slowly and quietly, as he shoves the last bite of food into his mouth. He watches the cops chatting and laughing with the women behind the counter as he chews.

She watches a fly crawling around the rim of her cup, stopping every now and then, coal black against the cup's sullied white, to rub its feet together in a disease spreading frenzy. A last hoorah perhaps, before the final lure of the purple light.

When he's done with his lunch, he picks up his serviette, wipes his mouth, glares at her, and demands to know where his coffee is.

Shit, she exhales. She forgot it.

A moment later, the old ladies stir. It's time to get back on the bus.

He gets up, tucks his shirt into his pants and his phone into his pocket. She grabs her handbag and gets up too. As she turns to join the old ladies, he grabs her wrist and yanks her back. 'Wait,' he demands, as he shoves his fingers through her hair and sinks his fingers deep into her skin. Her collar scratches the back of her sweaty neck as he squeezes.

They hang back as the women and cops file out the front door

She hears the zap of the ultraviolet light as the fly meets its fate.

Finally, he shoves her forward, commands her to get going, as he guides her past the tables and back into the blistering heat.

Outside, the hot dry air burns her lungs. He steers her past the cops who stand beside their patrol car chowing down on their fat-laden food towards the queue of little old ladies who are waiting to board the bus.

With his fingers wrapped tightly around her neck, he pushes them into the middle of the line. The old ladies behind them frown and purse their lips.

The line steadily moves forward towards the door.

Four and a half years of wearing his frailties like an old woollen overcoat that's patched and ugly.

Her heart starts pounding in her chest.

A step closer.

She can't do it anymore.

They're almost at the door. Finally, he lets go of her neck, but she hesitates to climb aboard.

He pushes her, snaps at her to hurry up.

She turns around to face him. 'No.'

His face darkens like a charcoal sketch. 'Get up there,' he hisses through gritted teeth.

Her heart hammers against her rib cage as she steps around him.

Furious, he grabs her arm, pulls her back, and hisses through gritted teeth, 'Get on the bus.'

She shakes her head, she can't get on the bus. If she gets on the bus, she'll die. 'I'm not going anywhere,' she says sternly.

The little old ladies ahead of her turn around to see what's going on. Several of them head back towards the door.

Furious, he yanks her close and warns her to do as she's told.

The cops look up, their attention caught by the commotion.

'Let me go,' she says, trying to wrench herself away.

'*Get on that fucking bus.*'

'Let me go,' she yells.

Pushed to his limit, he slaps her across the face so hard she slams into the side of the bus. As he raises his fist to have another go, the old ladies step in between them.

He clenches his jaw as he looks around and realises he's surrounded by a bunch of old women in white.

Then he sees the cops coming towards him. 'Shit,' he hisses, before taking off in a sprint.

She holds the side of her face as she stands up and looks at the women surrounding her. One of them, one of three she encountered in the ladies' room, holds out her hand. 'The bus is leaving, dear. We'd better hurry.' She nods and takes the old woman's hand.

They climb aboard the bus and the door hisses closed behind them.

She makes her way down the aisle and takes her seat. A moment later, the bus pulls out of the carpark and onto the highway. She swipes at a pearl of sweat that trickles down beneath her collar as she slides into the seat by the window. She peers through the dark lenses of her sunglasses as the cops shove him, handcuffed, into the back of the patrol car.

The bus picks up speed. They're on their way.

She nods as she leans back in her seat, grateful for the cool, conditioned air.

The Roos Are Loose

Drool pools beneath Brutus's jowls as he lies on the floor with his big black eyes staring up at Daniel who sits on the edge of the double bed tapping his fingers slowly, unconsciously, on the cold steel barrel of the .22 rifle that's propped between his bare feet.

Daniel watches Kelly through the bedroom window. She's in the backyard wearing paint-stained track suit pants and that raggedy old band t-shirt that she loves so much as she hangs laundry on the clothesline. Her long blonde hair hangs in a tangled mess over her shoulders. She's been up for hours but still hasn't found the time to brush it.

The kids are in the yard with her. Emma's sitting at the patio table pouring tea for her favourite dolls. She's got her mother's blonde hair and slender limbs. She loves school and her friends, and those ballet lessons... She hasn't missed a single one since they signed her up at the On Pointe Ballet School over a year ago. Daniel smiles, almost imperceptibly, as he remembers her recital a few weeks ago. He was so proud of her. She'd remembered every step, every twirl. But Matthew... Bloody hell, he's a handful. He couldn't stop fidgeting. The last thing he wanted to do was sit there for an hour watching his sister prancing around on the stage. He just wanted to get up and play.

Now, he's playing with mud. He picks up a huge handful of it, squeezes it between his plump little fingers then promptly lobs a gob of it at Emma. He laughs and laughs when it misses her and hits the clean white sheet that Kelly just hung on the line. Kelly throws a hand to her hip and barks his name, but it's hard to be mad at him when he smiles and claps his little hands together triumphantly.

A tear wells in the corner of Daniel's eye. He loves them so much, but he can't take it anymore. The pain. The fear. The nightmares…

The boxer dog flinches as Daniel wraps his fingers around the barrel of the gun and tightens his grip.

'So, how'd it go?' Daniel's father says, plonking the teapot down on the table in front of him.

Daniel remembers the teapot fondly. It was his mother's favourite. It's the one she used when special visitors came.

Daniel's leg jiggles at a furious pace beneath the table. 'The bloke was a prick.'

'What do you mean he was a prick?'

'He said my list of skills was limited.'

'What'd you say?'

'I told him that I've got lots of skills but that I can't put 'em on my resume because they're classified.'

'What'd he say to that?'

'He said he wasn't sure that I'd be happy doing administration.'

His father takes his seat at the head of the table then wraps his fingers, tremulous with age, around the teapot's handle and pours their tea. In all the years Daniel's been gone from home, nothing has changed. The same wallpaper hangs on the walls. The same cupboard doors don't quite shut properly. The same dishes sit on the cupboard shelves. It even has the same smell, the smell of musty carpet and brittle lino.

Daniel shakes his head. 'Twelve years, dad. Twelve bloody years and it all counts for shit. I've got all these skills that mean absolutely nothing. They're all bloody absolutely useless unless I'm in some godforsaken desert hunting down someone else's enemy.'

His father scoops a mountain of fine white crystals from the sugar bowl. 'Yeah, well, you've just got to take it on the chin and look for something else. You've got a family to look after.'

Daniel slams his fist on the table, sloshing tea over the sides of their cups onto his mother's old yellow tablecloth. 'I know I've got a family,' he shouts. 'I know I should be looking after them. Don't you think I'm trying to do that?'

The old man grips the teaspoon of sugar as he looks up at him in stunned silence.

Without another word, Daniel gets up from the table and walks out the back door, slamming it closed behind him.

'Yeah!' Robbo cries after sinking the striped blue ball in the corner pocket. 'What'd I tell, you, mate?' He says grinning from ear to ear. 'This one's mine.'

Daniel laughs. 'Yeah, well, I thought I'd spot you one game. Don't want you crying in your beer.'

Childhood friends, Daniel and Robbo have been coming to the one hundred-year-old Ballegie Pub since they were kids, sitting on their mothers' knees and sneaking sips of their fathers' beer. All these years later, the dank smell of decrepit wood and the fetid stench of the beer-soaked carpet are oddly comforting.

Robbo leans over the table as he lines up his next shot. 'Watch this. Fourteen in the top pocket.'

'I'll believe it when I see it,' Daniel says, smirking. 'I'm going to get another beer. You want one?'

Robbo looks up. 'We've been here less than an hour, mate. That's your third.'

Daniel bristles. 'Just shut your yap and take your shot.'

Robbo frowns but doesn't push it. He gets his eyes back on the game.

Daniel turns around—and slams straight into a punter who's walking past the table causing beer to slosh like a tidal wave over the rim of the glass in his hand.

'Oh, shit,' Daniel says. 'Sorry about that, mate.'

Furious, the bloke shoves his pointed finger in Daniel's face. 'I'm not your mate and you should watch where you're going… Cunt.'

Daniel's mind races back to Afghanistan where he's looking down the barrel of a rifle held by a Taliban insurgent. Right there, at that minute, a million thoughts race through Daniel's mind as he calculates the quickest and most efficient way to take the man out.

The next thing he knows, he can hear his name being called, 'Daniel. Let him go.'

The sound of Robbo's voice echoes in Daniel's ears.

'Daniel!'

Sweating and shaking, Daniel snaps out of it. He realises he's got his hand around the stranger's throat and that Robbo is tugging on his arm desperately trying to pull him away. The guy's face is bright red as Daniel's fingers sink deeper and deeper into his flesh.

'Daniel!'

Daniel lets go.

The bloke clutches at his throat as he gags for breath.

'Get outta here, mate,' Robbo says, pushing the bloke in the direction of the door.

The bloke coughs as he looks back before slinking out the door. 'The bloody roos are loose in the top paddock, that's for sure.'

Robbo frowns as he looks at his friend. 'What the fuck was that?' he says, aghast.

Daniel drags his fingers through his hair. 'I don't know,' he says. 'I don't know.'

Daniel swills Carlton Draught from a stubbie as he sits on the couch watching the Magpies trouncing the Bombers in the final quarter of the televised match. Emma's beside him, playing quietly with one of her dolls. Matty is on the floor in front of them, squealing as he smashes his toy cars together head on.

Daniel glares down at him. 'Hey, Matty, keep it down, all right,' he says. He knows the kids are just playing, but the noise. He can't hear the fucking TV.

Entranced in his game, Matty doesn't seem to hear him.

Daniel turns his attention back to the TV, just in time to see Collingwood's full forward leap onto his opponent's shoulders to take a spectacular mark. 'All right!' he shouts, sitting forward and pumping his fist in the air. 'Go, Pies!'

'Bam, bam, bam,' Matty cries out as he smashes the cars together again.

'Matty,' Daniel yells, 'shut up, I told ya.'

But it's no use. Matty's excitement has reached fever pitch. He pounds one car on top of the other, 'bam, bam, bam,' his voice jangling Daniel's nerves with every smash.

'Bam, bam, bam, bam!'

'Mathew!'

'Bam, bam, bam!'

Daniel grits his teeth and raises his hand ready to strike the boy. 'I told you to quit that fucking noise!'

Matthew looks up at him, his eyes wide and his mouth hanging open.

Emma clings to her doll.

Fury burns in Daniel's eyes as he glares down at the boy.

Terrified, Matthew's bottom lip starts trembling. A moment later, he starts wailing.

Emma leaps off the couch and runs out of the room leaving her doll behind her.

Daniel drops his hand, gets up off the couch, snatches Matthew up and holds him tight as he whispers over and over again how sorry he is.

Brutus sits in the kitchen doorway watching Daniel who stands in the hallway with his back pressed firmly against the wall. In the tunnel-like space, he can hear faint noises of the children playing in their rooms. The wailing of a battery-operated fire engine from Matthew's room, and the sounds of a make-believe tea party from Emma's. In the kitchen, he can hear Kelly talking on the phone.

'We've been waiting for months,' she says with a stern voice.

Then silence as Kelly pauses to listen to the person on the other end of the line. Finally, she responds. 'He can't wait another seven weeks,' she argues. 'He needs to see someone. Not next month, not next week. But today…'

More silence.

Daniel closes his eyes, aware that his wife is doing battle for him. Ashamed that his wife is doing battle for him.

'I don't care if his case is making progress! It's not fast enough. He needs help. He needs help now.'

Daniel turns and walks away.

'Look,' Kelly says with an exasperated sigh, 'I don't mean to be rude, but I don't think you understand the urgency here.'

Daniel knows it's a battle she can't win.

No one can win.

The sound of the receiver slamming into the cradle follows him as he goes.

On the edge of wakefulness, Daniel frowns and gasps as he stirs from a fitful sleep. Finally, he opens his eyes and realises that Kelly isn't in the bed beside him. It must be late. She must have gone to work. He can hear the radio playing in the kitchen; the community station. The announcer is talking about the Ovine Johnes crisis and the toll the disease is taking on local sheep farmers.

The voice gets louder as Daniel walks down the hall.

In the kitchen, the smell of burnt toast lingers in the air. Daniel goes to the fridge and grabs the carton of orange juice.

Tap, taptap, tap.

The plastic tassel hanging from the blind strikes rhythmically against the glass on a breeze that steals in through the open window.

On the radio, white noise seeps into the spaces between the radio announcer's words.

Tap, taptap, tap.

The tassel still swings in the breeze.

The announcer's voice becomes garbled military radio chatter.

Brutus sits beside him, starts nuzzling at his hand.

Daniel looks down at him, pats him on the head.

Tap, tap, tap.

The military chatter gets louder.

Helicopter rotor blades whir overhead.

And somewhere a woman starts wailing.

Daniel looks up.

Drops the carton of juice.

It hits the floor spewing liquid like a volcano.

On the other side of the room, the Taliban insurgent aims a rifle at him.

Daniel holds up his hand. 'No.'

The insurgent's finger twitches on the trigger.

The plastic tassel hits the glass.

Radio chatter fills the room.

Daniel takes a step back.

The insurgent pulls the trigger.

Daniel shouts and hits the floor.

Kelly rushes in. The kids are behind her. Emma takes one look at her father trembling on the kitchen floor then slinks behind her mother. 'What's wrong with Daddy?' she whispers, clinging to her mother's leg.

'Emmy,' Kelly says, 'take Matty to his room, okay?'

'Okay,' Emma replies.

Emma takes Matthew's hand and leads him out of the room.

Kelly takes a step towards her husband. 'Daniel?'

Daniel doesn't reply. It's like he doesn't even know she's there.

Kelly kneels on the floor beside him, slowly reaches out to touch his shoulder. 'Dan? What's going on, baby?'

At last Daniel turns to look at her, fear churning in his bloodshot eyes.

Kelly wraps her arms around his shoulders. 'It's all right. It's okay,' she whispers, as she wraps her arms around him and holds him tight, rocking him as they weep.

Brutus sits outside the bathroom, his nose pressed against the crack between the bottom of the door and the floor. Inside the bathroom, steam fills the tiny room, hangs from the ceiling like sinister stratus cloud. As the water cascades over his shoulders, Daniel presses his palms against the wall tiles and unleashes a silent scream, ripped from the deepest, darkest places inside his soul.

The smell of freshly-baked biscuits fills Louise Miller's house. Chocolate chip. Matthew's favourite. It's homely and strangely comforting. At the front door, Emma gives Aunty Louise a big hug while Matthew runs past them and straight into the kitchen compelled by the promise of sugary goodness.

'Thanks for taking the kids today,' Kelly says.

'That's all right, love. I'm happy to look after 'em. It's not like I've got anything else on. And they'll be good company.'

Kelly tenses her shoulders. 'I can't pay you. Things are a bit tight.'

Louise frowns, concerned for her friend. 'You don't need to pay me, love. Look, why don't you come inside and have a cup of tea before you go to work?'

'Yeah, okay.'

In the kitchen, Kelly sits at the table while Louise pours boiling water into the tea pot.

'So, Daniel still can't get a job, eh?'

'He's trying, but...' Kelly swallows hard. 'It's been two years since he left the army, three since he was in Afghanistan.' She hesitates. 'He gets so angry. And has these... Episodes. Emma's started grinding her teeth in her sleep.' She pauses, struggling under the weight of her confession. 'I don't know how to help him. I don't know how to help us.' She shakes her head. 'Sometimes I wonder if we'd be better off...'

Louise puts her hand over the top of Kelly's and gives it a comforting squeeze. 'When Jack came home from Vietnam,' she says, 'he was a different man. War does things to them. Terrible things. A doctor told me once that soldiers are taught to survive. They're taught to ignore their feelings. Then when they come back home, they don't see the world the way they used to see it.' She pulls a cup and saucer closer. 'He said sometimes it can take years for those feelings to come back again, and when they do... Well, let's just say a lot of marriages don't make it.'

Daniel walks into the house. It's dark and quiet. He checks the children's bedrooms. They're not there; their beds are still made. He frowns as he walks into the lounge room. Light from the television flickers in the darkness. The sound is barely audible. Matthew's toys are all over the floor. There's a glass of wine on the table. Kelly is asleep on the couch.

Daniel stands in the doorway looking at her. He knows she works hard. He knows that her shop assistant wage is the only thing keeping the family afloat.

He walks over to the couch and kneels on the floor in front of her. He slips the thin strap of her tank top off her shoulder and presses his lips to her naked skin. He loves the smell of her. The taste of her. A tear wells in the corner of his eye as he remembers the day she walked into the footy club. She was so beautiful... He was playing pool with some of the blokes in his unit. He'd lined up his shot then for some reason, he doesn't know why, he glanced up and saw her as she walked through the front door.

And that was it; he was smitten. His mates nagged him to hurry up and take his shot. He did, but he was so distracted he sunk the white then quit the game. The others complained, but he didn't care. He guzzled a glass of Dutch courage then walked over to the woman who'd just walked through the door and introduced himself.

Her eyes flutter open. 'Oh, shit. What time is it?

'It's late.'

He kisses her again. 'Where are the kids?'

'I had to work late. They're still at Louise's.'

Daniel nods then hangs his head.

Kelly frowns, concerned, as she runs her fingers through his hair. 'What's wrong?'

'I'm sorry,' he whispers.

Kelly wraps her arms around him. 'It's all right,' she says. 'It's okay.'

Kelly sighs as she drags the blade of the box cutter through the tape that secures the cardboard flaps. She jumps, startled, when the Andy the manager taps her on the shoulder. 'It's time for your break,' he says. Kelly frowns as she glances at her watch. It's almost eleven o'clock. She'd been so deep in thought... She retracts the blade and puts the box cutter in her pocket and makes her way to the staff room at the back of the store.

At home, Daniel sits alone with his rifle in his hand. Beads of sweat trickle down from his temples as the smell of animal dung and dirt, baked in the stifling heat, creeps into his nostrils, and the sounds of war, of distant and sporadic gunfire, fill his aching head.

Then, above the sound of helicopters and gunfire, he hears something else. Breathing. Faint. Intermittent. Laboured. Hyper alert, he grips his rifle and attempts to pinpoint the source.

He raises the rifle and sets off, ghost walks, heel-toe-heel-toe, into the darkness. The further he goes, the louder the breathing gets.

In the distance, a phone starts ringing.

He ignores it and keeps going. Finally, he spots a captured insurgent who stands with shoulders slumped, hands tied behind his back, and with a filthy hessian bag pulled down over his head. Great waves of fear and frustration and betrayal surge inside him as he circles the man, jabs at his chest, stomach, shoulders, and back with the barrel of his rifle.

The phone keeps ringing.

Furious, Daniel whacks the insurgent in the back of the knees with the butt of his rifle.

'Ahhhh…' The insurgent falls to his knees, his war-weary body slumped in pain and despair, his head hanging down.

The phone keeps ringing.

Daniel walks around in front of him, then rips the bag from the enemy soldier's head and tosses it on the ground.

'Look at me,' Daniel says.

The insurgent doesn't move.

'Look at me!' Daniel shouts.

The phone keeps ringing.

The insurgent slowly raises his dirt-caked face.

A tear hangs tenuously on the edge of Daniel's lower eyelid as he looks down at the terrified man.

As he looks down at *himself*.

In the staffroom, Kelly presses her mobile phone to her ear as she stands at the bench stirring a cup of cheap instant coffee.

In the kitchen, the phone on the wall rings and rings.

In the bedroom, Daniel grips the .22 calibre rifle in his trembling hands as sits on the edge of the bed that he shares with her and presses the barrel up hard beneath his chin.

He can't take this anymore.

The phone rings out.

He can't take this anymore.

The Hanging of Jean Lee

THURSDAY 15ᵀᴴ FEBRUARY 1951
Four days before the execution

The pungent odour of turpentine and beeswax, used to polish the pine wood floor, lingers in every hard-angled corner of the chapel as Sister Agnes kneels in a pool of pale lamplight, in the silence that's loudest before dawn, with her head bowed, her eyes closed, and her fingers woven tightly together as she whispers to God. 'I'm lost, Father. I've lost my way. I have no idea what I'm doing here. What am I doing here? What is my purpose? Help me, Father. Guide me. Please don't let me stray.'

At the end of her prayer, Agnes rests her head on her hands and sighs. She didn't sleep well last night. In fact, she hasn't slept well for many nights. For the last four months, her sleep has been broken and plagued by nightmares.

There are so many who are lost. So many who need their help. The Community's resources are stretched to the limit, as is her ability to feel sympathy for those she's sworn to help. She used to find satisfaction in this honest, down-to-earth work. But now... Now, she's not so sure.

***

The late afternoon sun beats down on the laundry's ancient brick walls making them hot to the touch. Inside, the windows in the large stand-alone building are firmly shut and barred. The lime render, not painted since 1921, flakes off the walls.

Steam rises in clouds from the boiling water in the massive coppers and is trapped in the arched ceiling creating an unbearable humidity. The nuns leave the outside doors open, but without a breeze the building is little more than a steam room.

Thirty-seven girls work in the overwhelming heat. Kathleen, the youngest, is barely thirteen-years old. She was sent here because her widowed father decided he could no longer care for her. And with no living relatives to take her in, this was the best he could do for her. Now, she spends her days in the laundry folding sheets and her nights in the crowded dormitory curled up in her cot and sobbing into her pillow.

At twenty-two, Edith is the oldest girl. When she was seven-years old and starving hungry, the corner grocer caught her stealing biscuits when her alcoholic mother neglected to feed her. Now a woman, Edith has the most responsible job in the laundry, ironing altar linen and the parish priest's surplices.

Other girls stand at the row of sinks that line the far wall scrubbing tablecloths from city restaurants. Some use giant mangles to press sheets for the women's hospital while the rest soak the sheets and habits that belong to the nuns.

'We'd better hurry,' Sister Margaret says, as she uses the long wooden pole to heave a soaking wet sheet from a copper boiler into the nearby laundry trough. 'It's almost time for the penitents to go to tea and for us to go to Vespers. You don't want to miss it again tonight.'

'I missed it once,' Agnes sighs, sweating profusely beneath the starched white wimple that covers her head as she cranks the handle on a giant wringer. 'In fourteen years, I've missed it once.'

Suddenly, Reverend Mother appears in the doorway carrying a linen laundry bag. Sister Margaret panics. 'Reverend Mother… I was just telling Sister Agnes that we'd better hurry if we want to make it in time for Vespers.'

Reverend Mother frowns, exasperated by the woman's zealousness. 'There's plenty of time before you need to be in Chapel, Sister.'

Margaret purses her lips, 'Yes, Sister, I'm sure there is.'

A short robust woman, fifty-five-year old Reverend Mother has been head of the community since 1918. Mother, father, teacher, confessor, she has guided dozens of wayward young women towards creating a better life for themselves. In return, her maternal need, powerful and undeniable, is quietly satisfied.

She hands the laundry bag over to Margaret. 'It's a donation of women's clothes. Be sure they're clean.'

Intolerably hot, Agnes rolls up the sleeves of her habit as Margaret sets the bag on a nearby table and plucks out a woman's frock. The pastel colours, stark against the drab colour of the laundry, catch Agnes's eye as Margaret holds it up by the oversized shoulder pads to inspect it.

It's an afternoon dress. A petite size. Made of polished cotton the floral pattern is light and summery. The calf-length skirt drapes over a pink taffeta petticoat. The short green sleeves are turned back to reveal pink lining and a pink belt hangs in loops around the pinched waist.

'Oh, my goodness,' Agnes says, reaching out to feel the fabric.

Despite some signs of wear and tear, some dull spots around the armpits, some mending around the waistline and hem, the quality of the fabric and the stitching is unmistakable. It's an expensive dress, designer, and from the faint odour of jasmine perfume caught between the warp and weft threads, it seems it was much loved by its owner.

'Sister Agnes.'

Agnes tears her eyes away from the dress to look at her Mother Superior. 'Yes, Sister.'

'As you know, Sister Ruth is unwell. I need someone else to take her place on care visit tomorrow.'

Agnes hesitates to respond. She wants to help, she truly does, but she doesn't know that she's got it in her. She doesn't know that she can find the compassion.

Reverend Mother frowns as she waits, senses the hesitation.

But a moment later, Agnes relents. 'Of course, Sister. Who will I be visiting?'

'Jean Lee. Her appeal to the Privy Council has been refused. The Premier has announced she'll go to the gallows on Monday.'

'Monday?'

'I hope I can count on you.'

'Yes, of course.'

Reverend Mother gives Agnes a small nod and then turns and leaves the laundry.

Sister Margaret shoves the dress back in the laundry bag and hands it off to Edith. 'You heard Reverend Mother.' As Edith walks away, Margaret grips the wooden pole and turns her attention back to the copper and the hospital sheets perking in the boiling water. 'What's the world coming to when they can hang a woman?'

When they can hang a woman, Agnes thinks. Hang a woman... Who murdered an old man. The thought tumbles over and over in her mind. What does she tell this woman? What does she say to her? How does she find the right words?

She goes back to wringing the sheet.

How does she find the words?

FRIDAY 16ᵀᴴ FEBRUARY 1951
Three days before the execution

Heat ripples above the tar on the road as the tangerine sun arcs across the mid-morning sky. Already oppressive, the heat of the day forces the acrid smell of blood and bone to permeate through the cab of the 1943 Chevrolet tray truck.

In the passenger seat, Agnes clutches the carpet bag in her lap as she almost gags on the smell. 'Do you mind if I roll down the window?' she asks Albert Gordon as they rumble along Nepean Highway towards the city.

'Go ahead,' Gordon says, keeping his eyes firmly on the road. A man of few words, he applied for the position of groundskeeper at the Community of the Holy Name after his beloved wife Sarah died of lung cancer in 1945, just three years after their only son Lionel was killed at El Alamein. Now, he lives in a cottage on the convent grounds, works seven days a week, and drinks his way through the long lonely nights without his family.

The rest of the journey is travelled in silence until they reach Coburg when Gordon makes a right hand turn from Sydney Road into Urquhart Street.

Agnes frowns as she looks at him. 'The main entrance is on Champ Street.'

'They moved her,' the old man replies.

The truck rumbles along the narrow road until they reach the south gate, a segmental-arched opening set within the wall and mounted with a cornice. Beneath the arch are two doors that can open wide enough to admit a heavily guarded truck.

'This is it,' Gordon says, pulling the Chevy to a stop.

Agnes rolls the window all the way down and waits as he climbs out of the cab to inform the guards she's here to visit one of the prisoners. She peers at the gate and the massive bluestone wall. Made from blocks cut from one of Coburg's own bluestone quarries, it's at least twenty feet tall and surrounds the entire prison complex.

The wall… Agnes can't help but think about the purpose of it. It's the same as the wall that surrounds the convent. The same wall that keeps the inmates in and the rest of the world out.

Lost in thought, she's startled when she realises Gordon is standing beside the passenger door. He turns the handle and yanks it open. 'I'll be back to collect you at three,' he says, holding out his hand to help her out of the cabin.

Agnes clutches the carpet bag as she takes his hand and slides out of the front seat. As Gordon walks back to the driver's side of the truck, Agnes stares at the gate.

How do I do this? How do I find the words? Dear God, let me find the words.

Then she holds her breath and steps into the world on the other side.

***

Perspiration beads on Agnes's forehead as she waits alone in the small reception room. Heat from summer's endless days, settles in the bluestone blocks that are coated with cream coloured paint. Suddenly, a female guard enters the room. She eyes the nun up and down, assesses her carefully before speaking.

'My name's Smith,' she announces. 'As soon as you sign in I'll escort you to see the prisoner.'

The 'prisoner'. She too has been stripped of her name.

Guard Smith eyes the bag in her hand. 'May I ask what's in the bag?'

'Clothes,' Agnes replies. 'I was told she could wear her own clothes.'

'Yes, but I will need to search it before taking you onto the block.'

Agnes nods. 'Of course.'

Agnes signs the visitor register while Guard Smith searches the carpet bag. She inspects each item thoroughly then stacks them in an untidy pile beside her. The final item is the floral afternoon dress. She holds it up, casts an eye over it, then proceeds to remove the pink belt hanging in the loops around the waist.

'Is that necessary?' Agnes asks.

'Don't forget to sign the register.'

Finally satisfied that Agnes isn't secreting weapons or anything dangerous into the prison, Guard Smith unlocks yet another gate and leads the way onto the block.

The clank of the gate slamming shut behind them echoes in the cavernous space in front of them. Agnes looks around. Light struggles to illuminate the building that opens out in front of them, but Agnes can see that everything, steel and stone, is painted with the same cream coloured paint that was used in the reception room.

'This way,' Smith says, leading the way down the wide corridor.

The silence is unsettling as they pass a dozen recessed wooden doors, a prison cell hidden away behind each one. And the heat. It hangs in corners under the stairs and the arch of the roof that towers above them. There's no escaping it.

Then something up high catches Agnes's eye. She gasps when she looks up to see a massive wooden beam spanning the width of the upper level. Agnes realises this is the beam that was brought from Melbourne Goal when it closed in the 1920s. This is the beam that hanged Ned Kelly. And Elizabeth Scott, Agnes Murray, and Martha Needle. Suddenly, the muffled sound of coughing startles her. Agnes tears her eyes away from the beam and looks at a nearby cell door. She hadn't thought... There are people in these cells. People. Prisoners.

'This is it.' Smith says, pointing through the dim light to a cell a few feet away.

The door of this cell is nothing like the others. This one has a door made of iron bars. It's an observation cell where prisoners are kept under constant supervision. Fingers gripping the handles of her bag, Agnes peers inside.

In the frail light that creeps in through the lone window set high up in the wall, Agnes can see her sitting on the edge of the cot, a cigarette burning between her bony fingers as she watches a cockroach scuttling across the floor in front of her feet. Lost in thought, she has no idea that Agnes is watching her until she scoops up the insect and carries it toward the bars that cut her off from the rest of the world.

'Step away from the door, Lee,' Smith commands. 'You've got a visitor.'

Jean stops in her tracks and looks up. The look she shares with Smith is one of mutual contempt. Agnes can see they're about the same age, but Jean looks old, worn, crinkled at the edges. Dressed in shapeless prison garb that's been worn by umpteen women before her, she's small, petite, and wretchedly thin. Her thick red hair, scruffy and unkempt, hangs about her shoulders in clumps, and she's got a fresh pink scar across the bridge of her nose. However, as haggard as she is, Agnes detects remnants of a physical beauty, long since faded, in the sensual arch of her eyebrow, the curve of her chin, and the slight downturn of her pale green eyes.

Jean grips the bar as she crouches down and releases the insect. Agnes frowns as she watches, disturbed by the tremor in Jean's slender hand. She's seen that kind of shake before. Involuntary. Irrepressible. It's the tell-tale sign of an addiction that lingers still. She watches the roach as it scuttles away beneath the barred door until Smith crushes it beneath the heel of her boot. The corner of Smith's mouth curls into a smile as Jean gets up. Jean knows better than to start trouble. She drags on her cigarette as she backs away.

Smith's keys rattle in the lock as she opens the gate. 'This is Sister Agnes,' she announces. 'She's from the Community of the Holy Name.'

Jean takes a seat at the small wooden table in the corner as Agnes steps inside the cell.

'Call out if you need anything,' Smith says, locks the door once more. 'I won't be far away.'

Agnes takes a deep breath and approaches the table. 'I hope you don't mind,' she says, placing the bag on the table. 'I brought you some fresh clothes.'

'You came all the way from Cheltenham to bring me a nice dress to die in? You're crazier than I am.'

Agnes ignores the comment. Jean moves the letter she's writing, and the photograph tucked underneath it. Agnes places the bag on the table. As Jean rifles through the clothes, Agnes looks around the cell. Surprisingly large, it's actually two rooms, one for the prisoner and one for the overseer. There's a kapok mattress on the single bed frame, two blankets, and a lumpy pillow. There's a lidless toilet in the opposite corner, and a hand basin on the wall. There's no privacy at all.

With her cigarette dangling between her lips, Jean holds up the floral dress to the afternoon light.

'It had a belt…' Agnes begins to explain.

'But the screws took it in case I got ideas about necking myself with it.'

Agnes doesn't answer but the hypocrisy of taking a belt from a condemned woman who might use it to hang herself isn't lost on either of them.

Jean tosses the dress on top of the bag. 'It's a little too high-brow for my taste. A little too 'goody two-shoes'.

'Clothes are an advertisement of yourself, of the way you value yourself. Your modesty. Or your availability. If you value yourself, your clothes will reflect that.'

'When was the last time you wore a dress? A real dress? A pretty dress?'

Agnes lowers her eyes as she hesitates, as she thinks back.

'Well?' Jean demands.

Agnes looks her straight in the eye. 'I was seventeen.'

Jean stubs out her cigarette, senses there's a whole lot more to the story. 'And…'

'May I sit down?'

Jean gestures to her cot.

Agnes sits carefully on the edge of the bed. 'I see you're writing a letter.'

Jean snatches up her pack of cigarettes and lights another one. 'You ain't gonna push me for some kind of confession, are ya?'

'I'm not here to judge you, Miss Lee. The law has already done that. As has the public. I think enough decisions have been made about your quality.'

Jean scoffs. 'My quality? I don't give a fuck what people think about *my quality*. It's none of their fucking business.'

'It is when you commit murder.'

Thwack! Jean slams a balled up fist on the table. 'I ain't a murderer, all right!' she cries. 'I ain't!'

Agnes gasps, startled by the outburst.

Then as quickly as her fury flared, Jean calms down and sits back in her chair. 'I didn't kill him,' she says. 'I was there when it happened, I admit that. But I didn't do it.'

'The law says that allowing it to happen makes you just as guilty.'

Jean drags on her cigarette as she sits back in her chair, her cold blue eyes scrutinising Agnes, analysing her, classifying and compartmentalising her. 'Yeah, well, the way I see it, it was him or me.'

'What do you mean, it was him or you?'

'I didn't give a shit about the old man's money. I just wanted to get out of there, but Bobby… It was driving him crazy that he couldn't find the wad of cash the old man bragged about.'

'Bobby Clayton's your boyfriend, isn't he? You confessed in order to save him.'

Jean looks away, clearly uncomfortable with this turn in the conversation.

'Why?' Agnes continues. 'Why help a man who beat you and sold you to others? A man who was happy to let you take the blame?'

Smoke curls from the corners of Jean's downturned mouth.

'Mr Kent didn't have a wad of cash, did he?'

Jean shakes her head. 'No, he didn't.' A moment later, she reaches for the photograph tucked behind the letter and hands it to Agnes.

Agnes takes it and turns it to the light. It's a black and white image of a pretty little girl. 'Who is this?' she says.

'My daughter,' Jean replies. 'She was seven when that was taken. I haven't seen her for a while.'

'What's her name?'

'Jillian.'

'She's beautiful.' Agnes holds onto the picture as she thinks back. 'My son...' she says. 'He'd be twelve now.'

Jean huffs. 'You... Have a son?'

Agnes nods. 'Yes.'

Jean smiles. 'Bit unusual for a nun, isn't it?'

Agnes nods as her mind jolts back in time to that day, to the moment she threw caution to the wind and gave in to urges, primal and ill-considered, that damned her body and soul. She'd seen him around the neighbourhood. He'd seen her, too. The way he looked at her... It stirred things in her, secret, indecent things.

One evening after her shift at the dress factory, she climbed down off the bus and began the short walk towards home. As she approached the dairy on the corner of her street she saw him. Her heart fluttered in her chest. She quickly looked away, but she knew he was looking at her, that he was peering at her from beneath the thick black curls that hung loose and wild over his dark brown eyes. He wasn't like the other boys she knew. The long sleeves of his shirt were rolled up past his elbows and he always had a cigarette dangling from his full lips. There was something mysterious about him, something dangerously attractive. She kept her eyes down and was determined to ignore him and walk right past him without so much as a smile. But, as the space between them grew ever shorter her curiosity betrayed her and she glanced up at him. He was looking at her too. She knew she should keep going, keep walking until she was safe behind the front door of her family's brand new Housing Commission house. But she didn't. She stopped and held her breath as she dared to snatch a look back over her shoulder. She was surprised to see that he had stopped too and that he was looking back at her. Her breath quickened as he took a step towards her. He took her hand and held it tight as he led her into the narrow lane at the side of the dairy. The stench of hay and horse shit crawled into her nostrils as she stood in the shadows of the overhanging branches and kissed him. She didn't even know his name.

'What happened to him?'

Jean's question yanks Agnes back into the here and now. And she very much needs to change the subject. 'Miss Lee…'

Jean's voice hardens. 'What happened to your boy?'

'I gave him up for adoption.'

Jean frowns as she stares at the holy woman.

'I wouldn't have been a very good mother,' Agnes says. 'It was for the best.'

Jean nods. 'My parents adopted Jillian.'

'Then you know she's loved.'

'Yeah,' Jean says. 'I guess I so. So, why are you a nun?'

'I think I've said enough.'

'I don't think so.'

Agnes hesitates. She's revealed more than enough to this woman. However, it feels good to talk. To share the truth. No matter how ugly it is. 'I'm a nun because I was alone. Because I wanted someone to love me. Despite my mistakes.'

'The nuns loved you?'

'No, they didn't. But God did. Or at least I thought He did.'

'You don't think that anymore?'

'Yes, but…'

'You took vows?'

'Yes. Of obedience. Poverty. And chastity.'

'Chastity?' Jean scoffs. 'How's that working out for you?'

Agnes frowns, suddenly furious. Who is this woman to speak to her in such a way? And how is it that she knows her thoughts? And those feelings buried deep inside her heart?

Jean sits back and looks Agnes in the eye. 'I did it 'cause I loved him. I thought he was going to love me. Forever and all that shit.'

Agnes nods. She knows what Jean means.

SATURDAY 17ᵀᴴ FEBRUARY 1951
Two days before the execution

Agnes rolls her neck as she stands beneath the shower of warm water soothing her aching muscles. The laundry was busy today and she worked extra hard. But now she has to hurry if she's going to make it in time for Vespers. She doesn't want to give Sister Margaret another reason to be upset with her.

She turns off the taps and steps out of the shower stall. As she reaches for her towel, she catches sight of herself in the small vanity mirror.

She wipes away the water that drips from her short dark hair onto her shoulders and breasts. Then she wipes it from her belly and the stretch marks that remain as a constant reminder of her wayward past.

Suddenly, thud thud thud, pounding on the bathroom door. 'Sister Agnes,' Margaret calls. 'It's time to go.'

Agnes's shoulders slump. 'I'll be right out.'

SUNDAY 18TH FEBRUARY 1951
One day before the execution

Agnes is on her knees with head bowed, her eyes closed, and her fingers woven tightly together in prayer as dawn light seeps through the stained glass window. She whispers to God, prays and prays for Jean's release from torment. She prays for her own.

MONDAY 19TH FEBRUARY 1951
The day of the execution

Swollen drops of rain splatter on the windscreen as the truck rumbles along Urquhart Street. It's the first time it's rained in days.

Albert Gordon flicks on the windscreen wipers. Agnes looks up as they scrape across the grimy glass, and gasps. Even though it's 7 a.m. Monday morning, a substantial crowd has gathered on the road outside the south gate. The crowd, mostly men, are divided into two separate groups, one on each side of the gate. The group on the right waves placards as they chant 'Reprieve! Reprieve! Reprieve!' The group on the right also waves placards but they chant 'Eye for an eye! Eye for an eye! Eye for an eye!' In between them, half a dozen men in suits and hats band together to talk amongst themselves. Two of them have large bags slung over their shoulders.

'Who are they?' Agnes says, as she watches them with concern.

'They're reporters,' Gordon says. 'From the newspapers.'

In a hurry to get inside, Agnes reaches for the door handle.

'Wait,' Gordon warns. 'I'll go in with you.'

Agnes sits back and looks at the fervid crowd.

***

Guard Smith guides Agnes along the upstairs walkway.

'Miss Lee's cell is downstairs,' Agnes says.

'She's been moved to a cell by the gal... She's been moved to a cell on this level.'

As they walk further along the walkway, Agnes glances down at the lower level and spots the prison's governor glancing at his watch as he smiles and jokes with several men in suits and three D Division guards. Clenching her jaw and gritting her teeth, Agnes looks up again only to see the hanging beam stretching across the void right in front of her. Unlike her last visit, the beam now sports a noose that dangles freely above the trapdoor cut into the metal floor.

'She's in here,' Smith says, pointing to cell 67A. 'The doctor's with her.'

Agnes stops, uncertain if she can do this, unsure if she can go inside. 'What do I tell her?' Agnes asks. 'How do I find the words?'

Unusually sympathetic, Smith considers her reply. 'I'm not a religious woman, but if I were, I'd think that God sent you because you're the one she needs right now and that He'll give you whatever words you need.'

Agnes nods, grateful for the woman's reply. Then she rounds the corner into the cell.

Jean, wearing the floral dress, is sitting on her cot. Her head hangs forward as the doctor, who sits on a chair in front of her, unties the tourniquet from around her arm.

Agnes watches as he presses two fingers to Jean's neck feeling her pulse. Satisfied he's done all he can for her, he gives her hand a plaintive squeeze, then grabs his medical bag and heads for the door, nodding to Agnes as he leaves.

Agnes takes a seat on the chair. Tears well in her eyes at the sight of Jean in the pretty floral dress. It's too big for her rail-thin frame, but a hint of her former beauty, unbearably faint, shines through despite the despair. Jean looks at the items on the bed beside her, an empty packet of cigarettes, the photograph of her daughter, and a hairbrush.

Spittle dribbles from Jean's lips as she looks up. 'I didn't think you'd come.'

Agnes smiles. 'You look beautiful.'

Jean smiles too. 'I do, don't I?' Then the smile slips from her lips as she points to a rubber undergarment lying on the bed beside her. 'They want me to wear that. But I don't think it'll go with the dress.'

Agnes frowns as she closes her eyes and hangs her head. Please God, let me find the words.

Jean lists sideways as she reaches under her pillow. She pulls out the letter to her daughter and hands it to Agnes. 'I didn't trust the screws to send it.'

Agnes takes it. 'Would you like me to brush your hair?'

Jean closes her eyes and whispers, 'Yes.'

Agnes picks up the hairbrush and gently untangles the knots from Jean's thick red hair. With each stroke of the brush, Jean slips into a world that is far beyond the here and now.

A moment later, Guard Smith enters and breaks the carefree silence. 'Sister...'

Agnes ignores her and keeps brushing.

'Sister, I'm sorry but it's time.'

The sound of clanking against the cell door's bars forces Agnes to look up. She gasps when she sees the hangman standing in the doorway in a knee-length white coat, a white felt hat pulled down over his forehead, and massive steel-rimmed goggles covering his eyes.

Suddenly, Jean's head flops forward, her body goes limp and she slumps, unconscious, into Agnes's lap.

Outside the prison, the protestors' chanting reaches fever pitch. Gordon stands on the street, leaning against the body of his truck when he checks his watch. It's 7.55 a.m.

Inside, Jean sits in a chair, the floral dress draping neatly over her knees. Her eyes are closed, her mouth is slack, and her hands are tied behind her back as the hangman's assistant slips a hood over her freshly-brushed hair. The chair sits on the gallows trapdoor.

An unnatural silence has fallen over the world inside these walls. It's as though the ghastly reality of the situation has only just dawned on those who stand present. Now on the ground floor, Agnes stands amongst them, the guards, the men in suits, and the newspaper men who have come to bear witness to Jean's demise. Her fingers are woven tightly together in prayer, so tightly they are white from lack of blood flow. Have mercy on her, Lord. Take her into your arms and have mercy on her soul. The hangman slips the noose over Jean's head and tightens the knot at the side of her neck just below her jaw. The hangman's assistant pulls down the flap to cover her face. The hangman stands ready, his hand on the lever, watching the clock above him. The minute hand ticks around to eight a.m. and without a hint of hesitation, he triggers the trapdoor.

Outside the south gate, Gordon looks up to see startled pigeons take flight.

Agnes stands still, frozen to the spot, unable to move, afraid to look.

Dear God…

Dear God, take care of her.

THURSDAY 1ST MARCH 1951
Ten days after the execution

A tangerine sun arcs across the southern New South Wales sky. Classic music plays on the wireless as Charles Wright sits on the porch reading the morning newspaper. Florence Wright rocks in her chair as she watches her granddaughter playing in the water spraying from the lawn sprinkler. No one pays any attention to the cab that passes the house until it stops and backs up.

The driver waits patiently as Agnes, wearing a white dress with a pink floral pattern, snaps open her purse and glances at the two letters placed carefully inside. One is from the Children's Welfare Department which contains information about her son. The other is Jean's letter to Jillian.

'Who is it, Charlie?' Florence wonders.

Charles peers over the top of his paper. "I've never seen her before."

Agnes pays the cab driver and shuts her purse. Then she takes a deep breath, climbs out of the back seat, and crosses the street.